THE WOMAN, THE JEWEL, THE GLORY

Revelation of the conquering strength and wisdom for the 21st century woman.

I0653440

Osayande Ben Edo-Osagie

Published by New Generation Publishing in 2012

First Edition

www.newgeneration-publishing.com

 **New Generation Publishing**

THE WOMAN, THE JEWEL, THE GLORY

Expose' on the conquering strength and wisdom of the 21st century woman.

Prologue

Acknowledgement

1. Anatomy of a woman

2. Dimensions of a woman

3. Spirituality of a woman

    i. Prophetic
    ii. Influencer
    iii. Church
    iv. Home builder

4. Challenges of the 21st Century Woman

5. Special tribute to my Mother.

Prologue

This piece of work themed *The woman, The jewel, The Glory*, is inspired by the grace of God and the life example of my highly esteem mother. The driving intent is to initiate a paradigm shift in the mentality of humanity towards women for maximizing an efficient living. The presence of Adequate insight and perspective of womanhood will herald a landmark transformation with preventive and curative solution to life question and issues. As we journey farther into the 21st century amidst all the complexities and challenges unfolding before our faces. The accurate and indepth understanding of the place and purpose of a woman as revealed especially in the book of proverbs chapter 31 is the key factor. The days of the great prophetess Deborah in bible history who delivered her nation isreal accompanied by Jael a fellow mate against the odds from the camp of the Canaan army. They where obviously helmed in and helpless until this judge of a woman switch on the gift of counsel and wisdom thereby changing the whole situation around. The lesson is that a wise man will not ignore the counsel of a woman especially when it sprangs from godliness. This historical conquest driven by a woman is the clue to relevance of an ideal woman, mother or wife in this age. The boundary that needs consideration is appropriate use and not abuse of the influence edge . The discipline of staying submitted and respectful to the headship of the man will certainly enable her fulfil this divine role properly and graciously for the good of the family, society and nationhood. Again, the stability of the marriage life is a booster, when the man is secured and liberated to acknowledge the areas of superior ability of womanhood. The path finder prowess of the woman, makes the mark in the life of a community. A typical example of the power and benefit of stability and role play in a marriage even when the woman seem to be at the fore, is the union of the Queen of England and Prince Philips the duke of Edinburgh. Their solid and consistent marital life has reflected so much in the prosperity of the nation in her 60 years on the throne as the monarch.

Acknowledgement

My profound and utmost dedication of this book "The woman, The jewel and The glory" is to my outstanding and beloved mother in commemorating her 60th diamond birthday jubilee. To God be the glory for a rewarding and fruitful life lived for the service of God and humanity.

Appreciation and honour goes to my father and legend of integrity and principles for the pass on effect of the grace to be an author. Truly like beget like. Also for his advice encouragement and sound wisdom

.

Special recognition also goes to my spiritual fathers and mentors in person and through their messages and books for their instruction, motivation inspiration prayers and nurturing in times of adversity. Certainly if I have attain any greatness it is because I have stood on the shoulders of great patriarchs and generals in the kingdom. These includes: Archbishop Benson Idahosa (blessed memory), Rev. Dr. Felix Omubude, Rev Chris Oyakhilohme, Pastor Ayo Oritsejafor (CAN president), Pastor Enoch Adeboye, Bishop David Oyedepo, Rev Matthew Ashimolowo , Dr. Mike Murdock Bishop, T.D. jakes, Brother Kenneth Copeland, Brother Jesse Duplantis, Pastor Jetezen Franklin, Pastor Paula White, Pastor Joyce Meyer, Pastor Benny Hinn, Papa Morris and mama Theresa Cerullo,Pastor Eastwood Anaba, Pastor Mensa Otabil, Bishop John Francis, Apostle Eunice Gordon, Dr. Mercy Ezekiel, Paul and Jan Crouch and the golden TBN family, Pastor Fred Igho (Kings Church) GOD TV family, Day star TV, Loveworld TV, Believe TV and Revelation TV. Furthermore the new generation of upcomming generals such as Dr. Ramson Mumba (EICC), Pastor Mark and Hannah Pease (EICC), Alex Omokudu

(VPA) Pastor Jerome Anekwe (Destiny Christian Centre), Pastor Oris onuwaje (kings castle church), pastor Banjo Oluwatula (kings castle Church), Pastor Bright Onoka (City of God), Pastor Tajh Onuwaje (USA), Pastor Amos Okafor (KICC), Pastor Tony Aisien (City of God).

Apostle Paul known as the man of letters, attribute his accomplishments in the kingdom to the grace of God (paraphrased). But I will say that If have been raised to the place of honour even as the journey continues by the grace of God, accessed and inspired through human source in the kingdom of God.

Likewise, the great feats achieved by the great king David in all his conquest was possible, with the help of loyal and trusted league of mighty men.

ANATOMY OF A WOMAN

The specie female known as woman (womb man) or the man with a Womb is a refined complicated and sensitive creature which was taken out of a man. This origin gives a clue about the nature of the female specie. The features and embellishments of a woman that graced her with an attractiveness and splendour can be attributed to the process and place of emergence from a man which is the rib a vital part of the human skeletal framework. The rib cage which is by the side of a man protects the delicate organs of the body such as the heart and liver and indicates God intent to make the man walk side by side with the woman and for her to be loved and cherished. The blessing of the creation of man encompassing both male and female specie seems to be more female specific as stated in the initiation blessing by God after creating man...... be fruitful, multiply, replenish, subdue and have dominion (Gen 1:28). This goes to validate the prophecy about the birth of Jesus which says the seed of a woman shall bruised the head of the serpent. The seed of a woman in this context speaks of Christ the head of the church. The structure of a woman potends the ability and grace to dualize the role of a man since she consists of the male and reason being that she was formed from the male. The feminine aspect is the tender nature in the mixture that makes great difference. The anatomy of a woman showcases receiving with evidence in her biological make up to justify why women crave for attention, affection and love. The capacity to receive and keep receiving affection can be outrageous. This tells of the depth dimension of a woman and why a woman can be very relentless in pursuit. The nurturing, fruit bearing and blossoming effect of womanhood is a major hallmark that makes her indispensable. This is representative in the birth of Jesus. The lord could not do without the womb of Mary but he could ignore the seed of Joseph.

DIMENSIONS OF A WOMAN

The dimension of a woman is a framework that deals with the physiological and anatomical structure of a woman. This explanation can be adduced from the scriptures or biblical perspective about some notable characters that were beneficiaries or involved in giving credence to this attribute of a woman. Solomon who was the wisest king that ever lived before Jesus emergence on the scene spoke and wrote much about the dimension of a woman in respect to the upper and lower extremities. Although Solomon was already out of touch with his relationships with God as a result of his indulgence with multitudes of women who shifted his heart to idolatry, yet he was still unveiling wisdom from his menace which is valid and relevant in our dealing in today contemporary world. Moreover the book of songs of Solomon was a shadow of the love between Christ and his church. Indeed all things works together for good to them that love God even to them who are the called according to his purpose (Romans 8:32). This truth was fulfilled because Solomon was a man that love God. The love of God made his mess a message to fit into the plan of God for posterity. What an awesome God. The romantic rantings of Solomon in relation to the upper extremities of the female analyses issue of the lips and the breast which are symbolisms in the light of biblical and natural reality. These are the attractive features of the female. The blessing that was discharged upon joseph in the book of genesis (Gen 49:26) speaks about the blessing of the womb and the breast. The womb speaks about productivity and fruitfulness while the breast is for nourishment, comfort and beauty. Seemingly Joseph possesses this qualities because you become before you overcome and the blessing on his life configured him to be an epitome of this values and attributes before he could exhibit or function in it. Hence, this blessing was manifested in his ability to administer Egypt through intense global economic recession and also ensure the survival of neighbouring and extended nations and his relatives and kinsmen which sought relief and reprieve in the prosperity of Egypt. This posture tells much of what a woman consist and how it can translate to practical solution in solving crisis. This also confirms the blessing bestowed on man in the book of genesis (Gen 1:28) after the creation. The pronouncement was dominion, fruitfulness, multiply, replenish and subdue. The capacity for the manifestation of this blessing is more tailored towards the feminine specie. This is justified by the makeup structure of a woman with the anatomy of the breast (the upper extremity) and the womb (the upper extremity). The pull of strength coupled with an emotional surge inculcated in womanhood is a recipe for enhanced results and outcome. The lip is a revealing part and aspect of humanity which the females derives warmth and romance.This truth also translate in spiritual reality the desire of God to relate with us intimately as prescribed in the book of (psalms 2:12). The feet (lower extremity) is another portion of the anatomy that attention is geared towards. Most women are hoodwinked with the fantasy for shoes and pedicures. The beautification of the feet is a major concern and a gratifying figure that most women tend. The spiritual significance of the feet is explained in the gospels. It says how beautiful are the feet of him that brings glad tidings and published good things (Romans 10:14-15). There is the natural inclination that women can very adventurous and resilient in seeing things through with a nerve for patience. Also, the tendency to reach and make contacts with people is a core interest amongst the female clique. This makes a woman a very efficient communicator of the gospel with the machinery of the feet to move and the mouth to speak which are areas of excellence as it concerns womanhood. The woman at the well of Samaria is a living proof of this testament (John 4:4-26). The encounter she had with Jesus made her a missionary of the gospel. When Jesus revealed her life history, she immediately went about to tell everyone what the lord has done for her. She became an emergency evangelist. The softness of the female also gives a clue to the sensitivity of the female. The is why a woman responds to touch which arouses her emotions. This fact was buttressed by Apostle Paul (1 cor.7:1) when he elucidated that it was better not to touch a woman before time...knowing that it potends consequences as it bothers on sexual chastity. On the other hand the positive consideration of this vibe of emotion is the making of an effective carrier of the message of hope and reconciliation with the requirements of sensitivity to peoples' plight. The template for this task is the high priest of our salvation Jesus Christ who is touched by the feeling of our infirmities and tempted as we are but without sin (Heb 4:15).

SPIRITUALITY OF A WOMAN

The spirituality of a woman is ultimately key in the explanation and analysis of the feminity she splendidly flaunts. The natural chemistry and make up she constitute gives a clue of the spiritual potency endowed in her. In the creation story we were told in the book of genesis (Gen 2:22) that woman was formed out of the rib of man, when he was put into deep sleep. The intensity of the sleep called *deep* and location of the rib explains depth and support or protection since the rib cage is known to be a framework that protects vital organs of the body. This scenario could give a pointer to the spiritual depth a woman carries and concour with the bible sayings that the deep calls for the deep (psalm 42:7) This is alluded to the knowledge that a natural thing is a lead to spiritual things. The woman specie is known to be naturally multitasking which is the ability to engage diverse things at the same time. The apostle Paul gave a spiritual reason to this effect that we can do all things through Christ that strengthens us Philippians (4:13). This is why a woman that is spiritually focused either on the positive or negative is a force to be reckon with. On the negative a woman that is sold out spiritually can do a lot of harm to humanity. This is so because a woman is more devoted to any task than men. The abundance of emotions she carries is a driving force. The prone factor to emotional issues also is the major traumatic experience women tend to face challenges mostly. An hypothetic finding carried out once said that a woman responds to emotions by 90% while men do by 10%. This raw findings if taken to considerations tell reasonably about the potential of a woman because the emotions when appropriately channelled can be a driver to heights and depths of great feats and results in all spheres of humanity. On the contrary when unbridled the result is heartaches with various ripple effects in homes, schools and workplace. Notably, infidelity in most marriages accrued from the failure to tame this physiology of humanity. But it is noteworthy that male folks are mostly culprits when it comes to marital affairs.

(i) THE PROPHETIC

The female specie called woman (the womb man) is known to be a natural seer or prophetess. The bible reference speaks of prophets as seers with the ability to see or discern and speak concerning things to come or past. The woman specie is graced with this ability natively. The coupling of the natural innate gifting with the spiritual endowment when she embrace Christ as lord and saviour brings the potency of this ability or treasure to full bloom and effect. The spiritual realization of her potential in the natural is the launching pad to the fulfilment of a glorious destiny through the help of the creator (God). This is noteworthy with the knowledge that the spirit profits all things. The biblical perspective has a lot of heroines with this prophetic grace in operation in their lives that enabled them to achieve great feats. The notable figures like Deborah who deliver her nation from the hand of the midianites as a judge. The prophetess Miriam was also a key factor in the scripture and she was Moses's sister. Also, prophetess Anna was a prominent figure with whom God did outstanding thing before the birth of Jesus Christ. She was known to serve the lord with fasting and prayers for a major part of her life. The ability of a woman to make things with this office has a more reaching effect than sometimes what a man can effectuate. The influence factor plays a major role. This is not initiating anyway women liberation as channelled by the world systems because a woman still has as place as the helper of the man who is the head of the home. Nevertheless women should not be sidelined or obscured from speaking out on issues that affects our social, political, education and family life. This clarion call need to be more heeded in the developing world where some still hold tenaciously that woman should be seen and not heard. This traditional philosophy that has been passed on from generation past has resulted in a lot of repressions and inhuman treatment meted out to the female gender culminating into severe forms of abuse and discrimination. This setback has somehow robbed our society of the graces and ability which womanhood has to offer. This can be likened to a rose flower that is trampled upon and results in the lost of its luxuriant beauty and contribution to the aesthetics of nature. Certainly, in an oppressive state or systems the ability or gifting of such recipient shuts down and relapse. In times past, down memory lane women used to be ostracized from speaking from the pulpit as a clergy or minister of religion. In secular quarters top and managerial positions where male colonized . The unveiling of knowledge has quelled this ignorance in the present day. The female specie is more alive to a prominent role of authority and responsibility in this present age and the outcome has been positive and pioneering. They have always been as good if not better than the male in service and management, is just that their operation as been channelled behind the scene playing support role for the men in their lives and pushing them towards excellent performance. The book of (Prov.31v23) agrees with this position by saying the husband of this type of woman is known in the gates when he sits amongs the elders. The insight into the future and prospecting as mentioned in (Prov. 31:18) is a landmark recognition of womanhood, particularly the virtuous one. As written in that scriptural reference, she considers a field and then purchase it perceiving that her merchandise is a good and wise decision. The gift of forecasting is being utilized in pre-planning and preparing for future goals and achievement. The aftermath of the good buy is hardwork and labour to ensure accomplishment of the dream and purpose ahead. This prophetic dimension of a woman played out in the case of a prominent feature in scripture called Hannah. The case of Hannah is that of a woman who was well favoured by the husband, which makes her more than ten sons to him although she was barren. Anyway, when she perceived and discovered the heart of God concerning her situation since God was in need of a prophet to replace Eli who was growing dim at the time, there was a change of Story. Her heart cry which synchronised with God's heart was reflected in her saying...*if you would give me a male child then I would give him back to you and no razor shall come upon his head and he shall serve you all the days of his life.......* *(1Sam1v11).* The product was Samuel a Foremost prophet of God who anointed Saul and David to Kingship authority. The prophetic inclination was also seen and utilized in the life of Deborah the fourth judge and prophetess in the pre-monarchical times of isreal. She was able to foresee and motivate barak the head of the army of isreal to victory via an unaware counterattack against the odds from the hand of king jabin of Canaan and the commander of his army named sisera.The workings of grace to counsel and the warrior instinct made the difference and defeated their enemies.

(ii) THE INFLUENCER

The word **influence** in the thesaurus dictionary is explained as the power of a person to be compelling or having an exertion or assertion over a thing or event. This force is a dominant trait and factor wired in the female specie. The whole framework and structure of the female also called 'Woman' exudes influence that causes or releases exertion or compelling aura over a person, situation or thing. This grace makes the female specie an indisputable voice in leadership hierarchy. While the male folk tend to lead by virtue of its position as a male the female lead by influence. This magnetic effect in the female has caused great feat to be actualised in diverse fields of human endeavour. However this gift of influence when wrongly utilized can result in the negatives. Summarily, it can build and also destroy. In the natural, it appears a paradox but with the spiritual perspective it makes a lot of sense which is relevant to bring a balance to our systems and world view. This certainly gives an introspect that the prophetic carries a great deal of influence that enables changes to be realized. The acronym in its syllable form **IN—FLUENCE** can be dissected as an in-nate ability that drives fluency. This scenario paints a picture of a speaking proficiency which is native with the females. Again, the prophectic ties up with this proposition because it involves words and speaking or utterance. The intensity of the sexuality of womanhood seems to have a spell binding charm or charis which is irresistible. This force of influence is natural with the general female specie but when the aroma of favour or the grace of God comes upon it makes a whole lot of difference and the channelling of this power has positive inclinations with a rub off effect. In bible escapades certain incidences shows the invaluable contribution of influence and the benefits it evolved. On the contrary there are cases where the inappropriate use has a sad experience. The story of Queen esther who assume the throne due to Queen vashti misbehaviour to the king Ahaseurus is a clear evidence. The favour of God upon her coupled with influence saved her people the Jews from the destruction already initiated by Haman. The influence of grace bestowed on her by God activated through spiritual exercise of fasting and praying caused the king to change the rule when it was against the law to approach her without permission. This is a case of the law changing due to spiritual influence initiated by the grace of God. The situation of Rachael is another proof of the pass on effect of influence that is godly inspired. The transfer of this influence that came upon Joseph is revealed in the sayings about Rachael that she was beautiful and well favoured. The verification of this blessing was confirmed by the pronouncement of God's blessing by Jacob on his children before departing. On getting to joseph he said he was a 'fruitful bough whose branches runs over the wall the archers hated him so much and shot him but his bow abode in strength and his hands were made strong by the hands of the almighty'. He went further to say the 'blessing of your father has prevailed above that of his progenitors and is upon him who was seperate from his brethren'. He also pronounced further that the God has blessed him with the 'blessing of heaven, of the womb and breast and the deep. The blessing of fruitfulness and influence is linked to the breast and the womb as deduced from scriptures, was passed on from the mother Rachael. The other negative episode of the usage of influence power was when potipher's wife wanted to lie with joseph and he fled because he feared God. This landed Joseph in prison enroute to the palace the place of promise. The contemporary world has some women that has left imprints in the sound of times both past and present through the release of influence. Margaret Thatcher the first woman prime minister in Britain was a pioneering factor in british politics. Indeed, she wielded a great change and revolutionise the polity forever. Although her reform programme was not popular in the island during her time but history has her name etched in Gold especially in Britain as a major key influence to the economic turning point in the nation. In the religious circle the blessed Mother Theresa of memory who was responsible for the care of the homeless and poorest of the poor in Calcutta India savaged numerous lives and left a legacy of mercy and love to mankind through her gracious influence. The queen Elizabeth 11 is also a major factor in spearheading a great and effective change in the realm of the British Empire. Her reign has witnessed the evolving of a prosperous and different Britain over several decades. The present chancellor of Germany Angela Merkel has played a lead as a key influence in the committee of women that have changed society. The posture of her toughness and resolute with a mix of tenderness and principle has emerged a better and dynamic Germany. The Aba women's riot of 1929 was a revolt led by about 25,000 strong women from the south eastern province who opposed draconian taxation levy imposed on them with a detriment on their business. This riot was the first to be heralded by women in West Africa. Nevertheless, the reprisal was the loss of lives to the tune of fifty women and fifty wounded. The resultant effect was the change of the tax law which brought about a turn in the fortunes of the women's economy .

(iii) THE CHURCH

The role of a woman as the church is an expression that is traceable from the bible. The bride of Christ which is the church. The head of the church is Christ the groom while the body is the bride. This revelation is obvious in the large participation of the woman gender in religious activities in comparison to the male gender. The pronouncement of God to Adam in the Garden of Eden after the deception of the serpent was that the seed of the woman shall bruise the head of the serpent (Satan). The product of the seed of the woman is the church the 'Ecclesia....called out one'. This prophectic utterance was fulfilled when Mary was conceived of the Holy Ghost and brought forth a child named Jesus Christ the head of the church. The woman specie has always played a pivotal role in church history. In the days of Jesus's ministry women where crucial in servicing the needs and responsibilities that were needed. The followers of his ministry consisted of women who greatly impacted and made invaluable contribution to reaching and meeting the needs available. Mary Magdalene from whom Jesus casted out seven demons became a key player in the ministry. The same Mary was the first personality to herald the resurrection of Jesus Christ from the dead. In the era of the early church after the upper room experience of the baptism of the spirit women were also movers and shakers even in an increasing measure. The likes of Dorcas a widow who was given to good deeds was a plus to the early disciples. The likes of priscilia was also a domineering effect in the ministry of Paul in putting Apollo right on doctrinal issues. The similitudes of the church being the called out one and the woman taken out of the man is a clue to the feminity of the church. The multiplicity and fruitfulness of the church is mostly driven by women. This is true to the findings that when you give a woman a vision she amplifies it with provision and it becomes her mission. The multiplier effects is just a part of the female constituent. In this last days women will be a key blazer of the trail in propagating the gospel and accomplishing major tasks and events in the contemporary world because they have the ability to make it happen. In the present day church world several women in the front line are making tremendous impact and bringing solutions to bear in solving human crisis. The like of Apostle Eunice Gordon is a pioneering matriarch's influence in women movement across the nations. The grace of God has enabled her to impact lives through the ministry known as Godhead prayer ministry and Spirit and life bible church. This grace has also brought changes in the reaching out to the needy and political circles. Futhermore, icons like Cindy Trimm an apostolic and prophectic voice imparting lives with her calling of prayer and mentorship in kingdom initiatives. Also we have Rev. Abiola Omobude a woman of valour imparting lives with the grace of God through Music and the word coupled with humanitarian achievements. Certainly as the we anticipate the return of our lord and saviour back to earth we will see tremendous happenings and arisings of great women turning the tides and effecting changes all over the world. The setbacks and limitations imposed on womanhood will be erased from mentalities. The prophetic declarations in the book of Isaiah which proclaims that the mountain of the lord's house shall be exalted and all men shall flow into it. This typifies receiving and embracing or welcoming into the sanctuary of safety and refuge. This is also a shadow and characteristics of womanhood known for the aura and belongings of receiving and homely in nature and essence. The woman led church in this last day of the church will be an enigma and sensation with all the paraphernalia of the glory and beauty of God at his disposal. This is foreshadowing the church as the bride of Christ adorned with the glory and splendour of Christ. This will tie into the promise of God which says he anticipates a glorious church without spots and wrinkles (paraphrased). The ashes will be turned into beauty. Indeed the hour has come for the woman to be more relevant and propagate the message of change and prosperity in our day under the structure of honour and respect for the man folks. This insight will align with the abolition of the curse of the law that sold away the females whose desire is to the male folk as proposed in the book of genesis. The last adam (Christ) freed us from the curse of the law which came from the disobedience of the first adam. Now in Christ there is neither male nor female, Greek nor Jew, bond or free we are one in Christ. There is no gender in the spirit but in the flesh inorder to be useful and functional on this plane of life .This was the original manuscript of God for humanity before the fall. The reconciling factor is Christ through the power of God. In him all things consist, Christ the quickening spirit. As we approach the coming and return of Christ to earth we will certainly become more and like him in nature, character, and work for as he is so are we in this world. Now in this cosmos world our revelation and insight about Christ gives us a foretaste of Glory divine before the final consummation of all things. This transformation process will be enhanced as we transform our thought life by the renewing of the mind. The best thing that can happen to us this last days is to behold him more and intensely through his word so we can become the word in flesh and dwell (to sit and rest

24

with a posture of authority) amongst men and the glory
they will surely behold.

(iv) THE HOME BUILDER

The function of a home builder is a major characteristic quality of the female specie by virtue of her nature and make-up. There is no denying the fact that if you give a woman a house she will make it a home especially when that woman is the godly type. A home speaks of a place of rest, solemnity and comfort devoid of all the distractions and hecticness or the hustling and bustling of everyday life. This role is specific and well detailed for the female gender. The female seem to favourably outdo the folk in this field of endeavour. This I believe is so because everything about the woman psychologically, emotionally, anatomically, socially and moreso spiritually just makes her fit to perform the task without any replacement. This goes to proof or validate why women tend to be more efficient in certain secular duties such as housekeeping and social careworker than the male. The home front is the woman's domain where she reigns majestically. This is attested to the fact that despite the career attainment of a woman in any field of endeavour, the homefront is the constituent of the heart. The true reflection of any home is the woman that resides in that home because she mirrors the whole lot that transpires. Moreover, her presence in the home is predominantly a booster to the sustainability of family life. The act of child upbringing is the classical and major duty and custody of the woman while the man has a contribution which is still very important. The nurturing from the cradle point to maturity, the female is just a round peg in a round hole as far as this task is concern. This invariably implies that a healthy society is a direct bearing from the home whose responsibility largely is shouldered by the woman. This will suffice to say that behind every successful home is an ideal woman. The act of building

26

is another functional duty of a woman. On the contrary a woman who is out of the moderating influence of the grace of God can utilize this endowment is causing harm and pain in diverse areas of human existence due to her strong influence. In this present dispensation there is utmost need for a God fearing and gracious woman to lead a well groomed and ideal home. The home cannot be a run down and rejected issue in the scheme of things in this present day and age. The consequence of the detriment will be obvious in society. As we gaze into the prevailing ills and vices in our present world we see a pass on effect of a failing home just manifesting on our street, schools, and work place. Certainly the balance of the male is vitally relevant to the proper training and education of the child but the woman in the mixture can effectively play out both role in an abnormal situation of the male absence and the children can still fare relatively well. In the balance of proportion the female absence has more colossal effect and peril than the male. Hence, every wise man should not take for granted the role of the woman in the home but rather appreciate and encourage her presence to the best of his ability to stimulate the excellence in the woman because women thrive on appreciation, affection and concern likened to a blossoming flower. This will bring out all of their energy, graces and intuition power to stir up that man and the home to pinnacles of success. In the area of religious and ministry every success in this field is traceable to steady home front. The peace and tranquillity in the home will rub off on the church. As the bible rightly instructs he that cannot lead his home cannot lead the church of the God (1Tim 3:5). However accountability and transparency starts from there. The branding of the virtuousity of a woman as characterized in the popular biblical book of proverbs (31 v10-31) is a true reference point as a proponent of woman empowerment gaining grounds in the present day for the betterment of the home as a priority and society at large excluding any iota of waywardness as often perceived by some school of thought. What makes this kind of woman standout is the truth of being an effective home maker and builder. The term idleness is expunged from her dictionary of life. The enabling strength and vigour she posseses is top notch. This drives her to rise early to responsibilities thereby providing meat for her household knowing that her constituency is firstly the home. The culture of time wasting is not her lot. The mentality and understanding of this kind of woman is that she knows the reason for her empowerment is to build an ideal and working home and family. This brings to the realization that any failed home can be traced to a woman who failed in her purpose. However within the context of the same Prov.31V10...*the saying goes that who can find a virtuous woman? For her price is far more than rubies.* The truth from this declaration is that this kind of woman tagged *virtuous* is not readily available amongs humanity. They are rare and mostly hidden or concealed and preserved for a specific assignment and duty on the earth. Her price is above rubies which means pearls or gemstone not commonly seen or acquired. This brand of woman is a gift given to special people, person or nation. She comes packaged with supernatural giftings and graces for the duty. In some cases or instances she is meant to raise godly and great children which will make history or impact on others towards purpose and destiny fulfilment and preserve a posterity on the earth. Again the word... *woman* was used in the verse 10 and not *wife* because her package *woman* is a man with a womb for the sake of responsibilities. This qualifies and makes her function and even play the role of the man when situations demands. The book of Prov.18 v 21...says he that finds a *wife* find a good thing and obtain favour from God. This gives room to choices and chances involved in the process of finding a spouse which is eventually favoured by God. The virtuous *woman* is divinely equipped with some celestial graces like strength.........*she girds her loins with strength...v17and18. She opens her mouth with wisdom......v26. The spirit of excellence is her virtue that seperates her from the crowd of many daughters....v29.*

CHALLENGES OF THE 21ST CENTURY WOMAN

The 21st century is a period of hyper challenges facing womanhood. The pressing demands and urgency of career prospects, family life and financial life coupled with the sensitivity and awareness of women's rights and priviledges in the secular, domestic and religious arena, certainly gives a vivid picture about women empowerment. In the ever increasing and fast pace changing world, the responsibility of women has evolved so much as to the level playing field with their male counterpart in diverse playing spheres or life pursuits. It just seems that a woman has transformed so much to the point of almost running the show while the male applauds the gallery. The dynamism of womanhood mingled with the graces of multitasking and sensitivity to issues based on her sexuality and influence has redefine the place of the womb man in the echelon of society and authority. However there are still pockets of sexism rants and discrimination here and there but it even disguises as a more driving and potent force that call for sympathy and favours to the female with a more stimulating vigour to excel beyond the norm and outplace the male. The corporate world in the present day has seen the best and the proficiency in women. Lofty Roles that once was the darling and exclusive preserve of the male has become their playing field. Moreover they seem to do excellently in the scale of preference than men. Particular reference goes to a colossus of a lady Ngozi Iweala who used her expertise as the world bank vice president to offset the debt of Nigeria running into billions of dollars. This feat was a cumulative effect of both power and influence which she wielded as a woman and result oriented one too. Again in the country of Nigeria another major icon is Prof. Dora Akunyuli who spearheaded the fake pharmaceutical products revolution in Nigeria and came out with a purge of the industry even at the expense of her life. In the global sphere women of the likes of Hilary Clinton who almost outpace the incumbent president of the US Barack Obama in the primaries And eventually became the secretary of state and the back bone behind her husband Bill Clinton's success in the days of his presidency. Also greats like Condoleezza rice the secretary of state in the presidency of George W. Bush was a brilliant figure that played key role in meddling foreign policies and bridging the gap between nations. The main area of interest as knowledge and development sky rocket in the 21st century is the balance of keeping a healthy home life and an effective social and career especially in a fast paced world. It is statistically proven that a woman heart beat is still the home front despite the successes in career and other endeavour. The ability of the Man to be a winner in the secular domain is anchored on the help of the woman. This is the mentality of God in the beginning when he said is not good for a man to be alone in the Garden of Eden. The blend of career and home is based on the good and solid help the woman brings in to the union. The dynamic ability and flexibility of a woman to rise up to the challenge in this day and age and be counted is fastly shaping the century. Myths and norms that bothers on stifling the progress of women are being demystified rapidly. The revelation from the scripture which says of this age and times known as the last days that 'have you seen a new thing on the earth a woman shall en-compass a man (Jer. 31:22). The light and understanding from this statements implies defence, facilitator/promoter and direction. The mechanism of defence been promoted by a woman will be represented in the home front and secular arena. She will be a shield and protection to the man in purpose delivery. The facilitator/promoter aspect of the woman will be a target in increasing the speed and execution of the dream and purposes of the man. Then as a direction she will be an effective counsellor and guide towards a safe arrival to the fulfilment of destiny of the man in her life. In a nutshell the 21st century will be one of achievements and feats in the situation of effective coalition of the man and the woman. The specially reserved home duty accustomed with women is undergoing a paradigm shift. Already in the developed world paternity leave is already in effect to allow the man have his share of parental responsibility involving baby sitting in the advent of child bearing and other domesticated duties. The role share is catching up with scriptural reality aligning with the reversal of the curse of the law which gave the woman away to ruled by the man. The present truth and revelation is that there is neither male nor female, Greek nor Jew we are one in Christ Galatians (3v28). The liberation of the woman is secured in the knowledge and awareness of their place in Christ especially in the third world nation. Certainly as we approach the return of Christ the king to planet earth the scriptural provision of Galatians 3v28 will be a reality with the woman folk paving the trail and setting the path with pioneering movements across the nations like never before. Recently, the number one seats of some nations were assumed by women such as Brazil, Malawi, and Australia. No doubt, there will be a numerical rise in the statistics this last day because of the divine equipping of a woman to be a better manager. It is noteworthy to say that a wise man should be considerate of this shift and position to derive relevance and honour from the female when she is exalted to lofty heights. Away with every jealous instinct and behaviour which sometimes creeps up when women lead the trail and the men follows. The prophetic agenda of these times tends towards the midas touch the woman specie has to offer from the kitchen and home keeping to nation keeping. This is the mind of God for the hour. Let him that has an ear hear.

SPECIAL TRIBUTE TO MY MOTHER

The woman, The jewel, The glory cannot be wrapped up without due recognition to my precious and iconic mother a pillar and tower of strength. A true and living testament of the book of (Prov.21v10-31). It appears to me that this biblical reference is personified in this woman of substance. This honour of recognition is dated back to the early years of my upbringing and developments which accorded me the opportunity to witness the valour and resilience that she possessed. My adorable mother whose name is Dora meaning......*gift w*as born into the ojeme family of Ewu in Esan central local government of Edo state positionally North of the state. She had a very humble and industrous beginning as a faithful steward in her uncle's house of blessed memory. She was responsible for the keeping and caring for the children of the house. Her stewardship was a trail blazer to greater things and grooming effects for future responsibilities that where ahead, concerning her own family. The affection she carries towards humanity was sincerely and purely a ripple effect from her own family. Truly as the sayings goes charity begins at home.

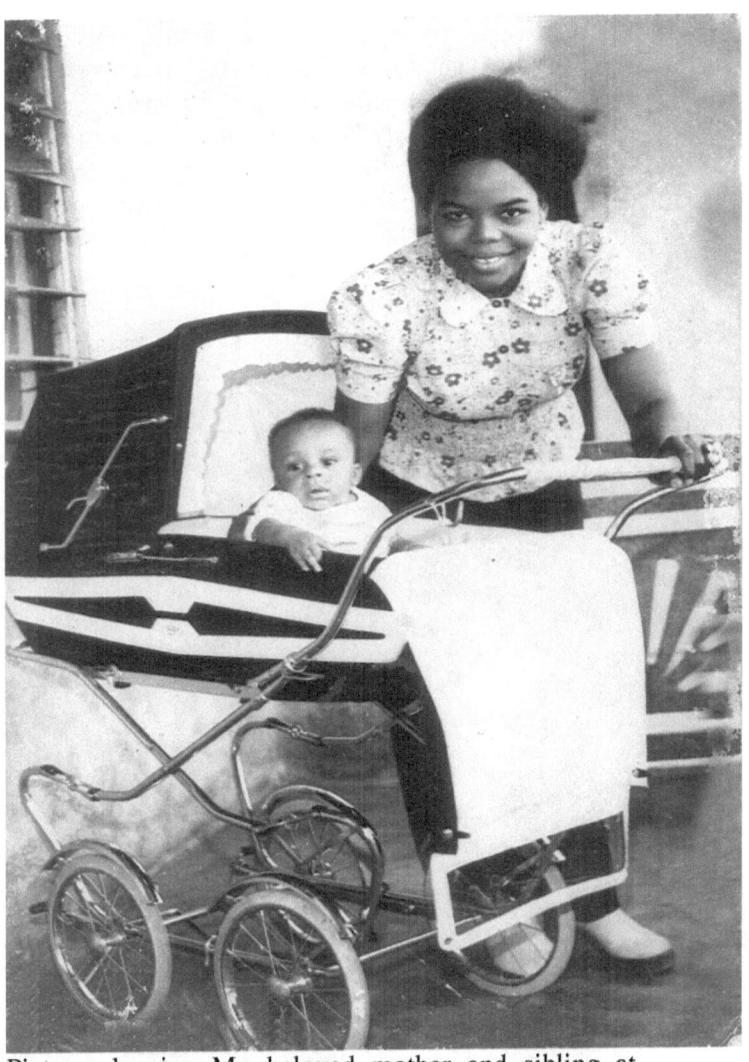

Picture showing My beloved mother and sibling at infancy.

Her apprenticeship as a seamstress in Singer a district company known for selling sewing machines and accessories, was a foundational platform for her personal development. Although not privilege to attain adequate and further education she resolved to be a celebrity and success in what she was involved. The follow up was laurels she won due to her productiveness.

Picture showing an award for a meritorious, loyal and good service.

After the stitch with time in her seamstress role in

singer a prominent firm in the 70's she then ventured into drinks and haulage business where she majored her time more and excel as usual. This economic provision and resources was a lifeline sustenance for the family at a critical period of our family due to my father's work crisis owing to detractors that were envious of his place and rising profile and so set him up with false allegations. The training of her upbringing came to the fore during this dispensation which goes to validate the saying that when opportunity and preparation meet success is inevitable. In this tough time, I and my elder brother were drafted into the trade in our teens. Then it was an issue of necessity alluded to the pressure in the home front. Although, I was still attending school But I had to keep up with the business, duties for survival. Nevertheless, this were times of grooming I had to endure. In this period of intense task in the home and business she was still bearing children even to the number of eight, indeed she was an epitome of strength and courage. She is really likened to a stallion in his fullness of majestic vigour and prowess. This enabled her to prominently raised eight children to maturity and higher education coupled with my father support. Inspite of this arduous and numerous responsibilities, she also was a generous giver and a committed worker in the church. Also, the leadership abilities she wields seems to be native and natural in her. Despite her educational deficiency, folks assumed her in the place of a school principal because of her natural giftings and wisdom in tackling life issues. Within the circle of friendship, she is a smooth and natural socialite, she is a people's person and an organizer of great repute in events and other family functions. In terms of loyalty and faithfulness, she has been tested and trusted. She is a sticker with people and she is always moved with compassion with the challenges of the needy and oppressed. An open hearted woman and really the law of magnetism in the 21 irrefutable law of leadership by John Maxwell which says like attract like is a reality in the aspect of marriage since my beloved mother got married to her compatible kind in this respect who will go his out of way for the betterment of others. On the social cadre she was up to the task. The ease and frictionless way she gets along with people where amazingly outstanding. Moreover, she is an ideal and good team player with a great likeability factor and respect .Her humility and calmness is the key to this feat.

Picture showing my beloved mother and her associates at singer.

In the area of spirituality, she was a role model who nurtured her children in the things of God. The leading by example was a guide she exhibited before the very eyes of her kids. The zeal and fervour was so contagious and inspiring. Her attribute for hardwork and unrelenting drive enabled her to fulfil and accomplish task that were entrusted to her care with ease.

Picture showing my beloved mother, supervisors

and work colleagues on inspection.

This unusual divine energy she emits is also alluded to the reason and ability behind her easy child bearing. In those days of child bearing, I could still remember vividly how she usually leave for the labour ward from her business place to put to bed just like the Hebrew women. This occurrence and several other observations like great health makes me to draw a conclusion about the enormous grace of God on her life. The likeability factor she carries even in the maternity ward is so strong and compelling. However, she is so discreet and sensitive in her approach of life issues and situations. The virtuousness of her character is a rare value that can be easily found this day and age. As the scriptures rightly put it a virtuous woman who can find her price is worth more than the rubies. I can say from the position of this provision in the bible that Only God can give such a wife to a man and it will take some details and qualities from the man and mainly purpose to attract such benefit from God. The other premise on which such precious jewel is released and deliver to a man is when the fruits of such union will be special and peculiar. As in the case of Mary and Joseph whose union brought about the messiah although apart from the contribution as in the manner of men but empowered by the holy ghost . God needed joseph for the caretaker role towards the child. Another scenario is that of Hannah and elkannah whose union produced a prophet of unrivalled greatness in the old dispensation of scriptures. The prevailing prayers of Hannah for the quest of a child in line with the will of God released the request of her heart. Her prevailing wisdom in the times of crisis and issues relevant to the family and in broader circles of life was commendably outstandingly. The flow of godly wisdom which she carries and graced in her has brought relief to many and families at large.

This ability was also enhanced and increased because of her loyalty and service to God and people. In any circle of responsibilities where she functioned whether religious or social circles, she is the propelling wheel that drives the results and achievements and most times she seems to be behind the scenes churning out the wisdom for the accomplishment. Despite the educational deficiency you could not tell due to the huge endowment and ability to relate with people. The exposures, association and willingness to learn and serve was a polishing effect to emerge the hidden diamond in her person. Her fighting spirit and humility was absolutely major in building the home front and improving the lives of her children at a critical time when my father was unable to meet the responsibilities due to sabotage and machination of men to derail his career During this critical time of our developments she stood like a colossus to blaze the trail stooping to conquer the odds. It was at this time of history that the tenacity and resilience in me was cultivated considering the enormous assignments of engaging and involving in my mother's business. Despite the intensity of the responsiblity of coping with school and work, divine providence was fair to me in still making excellent grades in my academic pursuits. Infact, of all my siblings I was so attached to the apron string of my mother. Her heart seem to beat in mine. She loves her children so much and still does and have paid a lot of sacrifices to see that they excel in life. The injunction of the scriptures which says you shall love the lord your God with all your hearts, soul and mind and then your neighbour as yourselves (Luke 10 v27) is a practical reality in her living. The people associating with her has received in small and big dimensions the spill over effect of the love of God that spreads abroad in her heart by the holy ghost (Romans 5:5). The compassion towards the helpless was evident in several circumstances even to a fault and as usual in the happenstance of the good, the bad, and the ugly experiences, she still maintains her goodness notwithstanding the eventuality of the circumstance . The reflection of a true and worthy amazon is the best explanation of her quality. She was much attached and endeared to her own mother and my grandmother ensuring that she was well tended and taken care of even to the last day of her sojourn on earth and no coincidence but divine arrangement that she stayed with my mother before the passing on to glory and leaving behind deposits of blessings before her departure. Her ability and ideal in the sanctity and respect for the marriage institution is unshakable. The three decades of her marriage life has seen tough times and storms but the tenacity of her resolve to stay put and weather the crisis is unwavering.In times when circumstance thrust on her the onus of providence for the nuclear family she indeed step up to the plate with a large heart and humility knowing her place and position in the union. The overflow of such magnanimity which she carries was felt even in the borders of extended family members on both spectrum of the maternal and paternal divide. The openness of her ways and the audacity to celebrate others is so profound. She sincerely wishes others so well with impunity. If there is any individual I can boldly and unequivocally state that has no rivalry or envious spirit then this woman of inesteemable value is the one. The nature of sacrificial approach to duty and the welfare to others is so consistent in her personality. The apetite for work and chores is her delight. The nudge against complain or squalm at any task is just amazing. Truly the Greek explanation rendering of her name "**Dora**" meaning gift of God is a living reality and manifestation for the benefit of many. The nurturing effect and perseverance spirit in her personality is key to her coping skills with people and situations. This grace also made it possible for her to adequately cater for her immediate and extended family, during the years of great challenges and difficulty resulting from her being responsible mainly for the upkeep of the home front due to the setback of my father in his work place. The size of the family of ten not withstanding she blaze the trail like a colossus with a charitable heart, consideration and wisdom which is unparalleled. On flashback and reflection of those days of huge task I cannot but say "amazing grace".